and forth the ball flew until Henry's hands began to tingle from the smack of leather against them.

"Throw it to me once more," called Scooter, "and then let's go down to the empty lot and practice kicking."

Henry wished he could carry the ball, but after all it did belong to Scooter. He gripped it firmly and drew it back over his shoulder. This time he was going to throw a perfect pass, the kind he had seen All-Americans make in newsreels.

As he started to bring his arm forward, Ribsy gave a sudden bark. Henry looked around at Ribsy, but his arm kept on going. The ball left his fingers.

At that instant a car whizzed around the corner. Scooter yelled, "Hey! Look out!"

It was too late. There was nothing Henry could do. The speeding car did not slow down, and for one terrible moment he thought the ball was going to hit the driver. Instead it sailed into the rear window, bounced against the closed window on the other side of the car, and then fell inside. The car raced on down the street and screeched around a corner on two wheels.

The football was gone!

The boys stared after the car. Henry was so surprised he stood there with his arm in the air. When he finally remembered to bring it down, he was still speechless.

"My football!" exclaimed Scooter. He stopped looking down the street after the departed car. He looked at Henry. "My ball is in that car," he said accusingly.

"Yeah, I guess it is." Henry was uncomfortable. "Maybe the man in the car will bring it back in a little while," he said hopefully.

"He'd better," said Scooter grimly.

The boys sat down on the curb to wait.

"Boy, I bet he was going eighty miles an hour!" said Henry.

"I couldn't even see his license plates."

"He ought to be arrested," said Henry, who was anxious to talk about anything but Scooter's football.

"He might kill somebody," said Scooter.

The boys waited and waited. The longer they waited, the more angry Scooter looked. "I don't think that car is going to come back," he said finally. "It's all your fault. You threw the ball."

"Yes, I know," admitted Henry, "but it wasn't my fault that Ribsy barked and that old car came by just then."

"You shouldn't have thrown it." Scooter scowled darkly.

"I couldn't help it." Henry scowled back. "I didn't even see the car until after I threw the ball. I couldn't catch it after I had thrown it, could I?"

"I don't care! You would have heard the car coming if that dumb dog of yours hadn't made so much noise. He wasn't even barking at anything. You lost my new ball and you're going to have to buy me a new one. If you don't I'll—I'll . . ." Scooter wasn't quite sure what he would do, so he didn't finish the sentence.

Henry didn't know what to say. It did not seem right that he was to blame. Still, half an hour ago Scooter had a new football. Now it was gone and Henry had been the last one to touch it.

"I have forty-six cents and three milk bottles you could have," said Henry hopefully. He hated to see that football disappear almost as much as Scooter did.

"That isn't enough," said Scooter. "You'll have to buy me a new football before next Saturday or I'll tell my dad and he'll tell your dad and then you'll really get it."

Henry suspected Scooter was right. He probably would get it. Once when he had accidentally broken another boy's roller skate, his father had given him a talking to and then made him spend his allowance to have it fixed. "O.K." he said. "I'll get you a new football. I don't know how but I guess I'll manage."

Henry turned and went slowly into the house. Ribsy followed him. "Now see what you've done," Henry said. "And after I spent my football money for your license and your collar and your dish, too." Ribsy hung his head.

Now Henry was just twice as far from owning a real cowhide football with nylon stitching and buckskin lacings as he had been half an hour ago. He was quiet the rest of the afternoon and all through dinner. He was thinking.

"How about another piece of gingerbread?" his father asked.

"No, thank you," said Henry absent-mindedly. "May I be excused, please?"

"Why, Henry, don't you feel well?" Mrs. Huggins was surprised. Henry usually ate two pieces of gingerbread and a third if she let him.

"Oh sure, I feel all right," said Henry and went out to sit on the front steps. Ribsy lay on the step below and dozed with his head on Henry's foot.

"Good old Ribsy, even if you did get me into trouble," said Henry.

He listened to the whish-click, whish-click of the water sprinkler next door and wondered how he was going to earn thirteen dollars and ninety-five cents in one week. He thought and thought.

He could collect old tin foil. No, that would take too long. Junk men didn't want the little wads of tin foil that came from old cigarette packs. They wanted big pieces that were too hard to find.

Maybe he could ask the neighbors for old papers and magazines. No, he had already collected all he could find for a school paper drive the week before. Besides, the junk men paid only half a cent a pound.

He could open a lemonade stand by the park, but lemonade stands were just kid stuff. Mothers and fathers were the only people who really spent any money for lemonade.

He could charge fifty cents for mowing lawns. That would be a dollar for two lawns. He would have to mow twenty-eight lawns to earn thirteen dollars and ninety-five cents. Even if he could get twenty-eight lawns to mow, he didn't see how he could find time after school.

As the evening grew darker, Henry still sat on the steps thinking and listening to the whish-click, whish-click of the water sprinkler. Whish-click, whish-click. Then Mr. Hector Grumbie, who lived next door, came out of the house and shut off the water. Henry liked Mr. Grumbie but he wasn't so sure about Mrs. Grumbie. She sprinkled Doggie-B-Gone on her shrubbery, and Ribsy disliked the smell very much.

Henry noticed that Mr. Grumbie had a flashlight in one hand and a quart fruit jar in the other. Mr. Grumbie set the jar on the sidewalk, tiptoed onto the lawn, flashed his light on the grass, bent over, and pounced on something. Then he picked it up and put it into the jar. It was too dark for Henry to see what it was.

The next time Mr. Grumbie pounced, he didn't put anything into the jar. Henry heard him mutter, "Oops, that one got away."

Henry couldn't stand it any longer. He had to know what Mr. Grumbie was doing. He walked across his own lawn and peered over the rosebushes.

"If you come any closer," said Mr. Grumbie, "you'd better tiptoe. I don't want to scare them away."

"Scare what away?" asked Henry.

"Night crawlers," said Mr. Grumbie.

"Night crawlers!" exclaimed Henry. "What are night crawlers?"

"Worms," said Mr. Grumbie. "Great big worms. Do you mean to say you've lived here all these years and never seen a night crawler?"

"No, I haven't," answered Henry. "How big are they?"

"Oh, about seven to ten inches long."

"Golly!" Henry could hardly believe it. "Ten inches long! I didn't know worms came that big."

"Here's one." Mr. Grumbie swooped and held up a worm in the beam of his flashlight. It was a big fat worm. It was at least nine inches long and as big around as a pencil.

"Wow!" said Henry. It was hard to believe, but there it was. Mr. Grumbie put it into the jar.

"Do you use them to catch fish?" asked Henry.

"That's right." Mr. Grumbie pounced again.

"What kind of fish?"

"Some kinds of trout, salmon, perch, catfish—

different kinds of fish. I'm going salmon fishing in the Columbia River in the morning."

Henry thought this over. "Do you always catch worms at night?"

"Yes. They only come out at night when the ground is wet. I give the lawn a good soaking so they'll come up to the top. Then I turn on the light and grab them quick before they have a chance to pull back into the ground."

Mrs. Grumbie stepped out on the porch and called to her husband. "Hector, if you expect me to have a lunch ready for you to take fishing at three o'clock in the morning, you'd better go to the store for a loaf of bread right now before it closes."

"All right. In a minute." As his wife went back into the house, Mr. Grumbie said to Henry, "How would you like to earn some money?"

"Catching worms? I'll say I would!"

"I'll pay you a penny apiece for every night crawler you catch."

"Golly," said Henry. "A penny apiece! How many do you want?"

"As many as you can catch. If I can't use them, some of the other men can." He handed Henry the jar and the flashlight, got into his car, and drove away.

A penny apiece! There were one hundred pennies in a dollar, so it would take one thousand three hundred and ninety-five worms to pay for the football. And forty-one worms for the tax!

Henry went around the rosebushes and tiptoed across the grass. Because of the Doggie-B-Gone, Ribsy stayed on his own side of the rosebushes. Henry turned on the flashlight and sure enough, there on the grass was the end of a big fat worm. But when Henry bent to pick it up, it was gone.

He tiptoed farther across the grass and turned on the light again. This time he moved faster. He grabbed the end of the cold slippery worm. The other end was already in the ground. Henry pulled and the worm pulled. The worm stretched.

It grew longer and thinner until it snapped out of Henry's hand and disappeared into the ground.

"Ugh!" said Henry.

The next time he moved still faster. He pounced on the worm before either end had a chance to get in the ground. He caught it! That's one penny, he thought.

After that it was easier. He caught most of the worms on the first pounce. Pretty soon he had caught sixty-two worms. Then he discovered he was running out of worms. Either he had caught all of Mr. Grumbie's worms or they had felt him walking around on the ground and had retired for the night. And he hadn't earned enough to pay for the football.

Just as Henry was wondering where he could find more worms, Mr. Grumbie came back from the store. "I caught sixty-two worms for you," said Henry.

"Sixty-two! That's great!" Mr. Grumbie reached into his pants pocket and brought out a handful of change. He picked out a fifty-cent piece, a dime, and two pennies and gave them to Henry.

"Thank you," said Henry politely. He wished he had caught more worms.

Mr. Grumbie started to go into the house and then stopped. "Say, Shorty," he said to Henry, who was going back through the rosebushes, "I'll tell you what you can do. Sunday morning I'm going fishing with a bunch of men from my lodge. Quite a few of us are going and we can use all the worms you can catch. Tomorrow night you get someone to help you and catch enough for all of us."

"Sure," said Henry eagerly. "I'll catch hundreds of worms for you."

"Swell! We can use them," answered Mr. Grumbie as he went into the house.

Henry sat down on his front steps again. Because he needed so much money, he knew he would have to catch all the worms himself. That meant he would need a lot of wet lawn. His mother would be pleased, even surprised, to have him water the lawn, but his lawn and the Grumbies' lawn wouldn't be enough. Maybe he could ask all the people on the street to water their yards Saturday evening. However, if he did that, Beezus and Robert and the other kids would ask what he was doing. Henry was afraid they would want to earn money catching worms, too. He knew Beezus would want to. She was the kind of girl who would like catching worms.

Henry sat on the steps wishing he had acres and acres of wet lawn. He thought and thought about millions of wet green blades of grass with big fat worms peeping out from under them. The park! Of course, that was it! It was only a few blocks away and because September had been unusually warm this year, the grass in the park was watered every day. If his mother would let him stay up later than nine o'clock, he knew he could catch enough worms to pay for the football.

Henry went into the living room where his

mother was knitting an Argyle sock.

"Mom, could I stay up later tomorrow night?" Henry told his mother the whole story.

Mrs. Huggins put down the sock. "Henry," she sighed, "how do you manage to get yourself into such messes?"

"Well, gee," said Henry, "I didn't do anything. I just threw this football and . . ."

"Yes, you told me," his mother interrupted. "Yes, you may stay up tomorrow night, but for goodness' sake, Henry, after this do be careful with other people's belongings."

Saturday was an anxious day for Henry. He wanted to avoid Scooter, but he also wanted to go to the park to make sure the grass was being watered. Unfortunately, he had to pass Scooter's house to reach the park. He walked on the other side of the street, but Scooter was in his front yard tightening the chain on his bicycle.

He shook his fist at Henry and yelled, "You get me that ball or I'll fix you!"

"You and who else?" Henry yelled back and kept on going. When he reached the park he was relieved to hear the swish of the sprinklers and see water spraying over the grass. He would earn thirteen dollars and ninety-five cents before he went to bed that night.

That evening Henry didn't wait for dessert. He borrowed his father's flashlight and several old mayonnaise jars and ran down the hill to the park. It was a warm night and the tennis courts and swimming pool were floodlighted. It was only beginning to get dark, but Henry hoped it might be dark enough under the bushes to start catching worms. He couldn't afford to waste time.

He passed the playground where he heard the children's shouts and the clank and clang of the rings and swings. Henry didn't stop. He had work to do. He went to the edge of the park where there were no lights and turned on his flashlight. Sure enough, there in the grass under a bush was a night crawler. Henry nabbed it and put it into his jar. Then he caught another. He caught worm after worm. Four hundred thirty-one, four hundred thirty-two, four hundred thirty-three. Henry was tired of pouncing. Henry was tired of worms.

When the lights of the swimming pool went off, Henry was still working. By the time that the lights at the tennis courts went off, Henry was very, very tired of worms. But he kept on. When he had added the one thousand one hundred and third worm to his collection he heard someone calling, "Henry! Henry! Where are you?" It was his mother.

"Here I am." As Henry stood up to rest his aching back, he saw his mother and father walking along the path.

"My goodness, Henry," Mrs. Huggins exclaimed. "Haven't you caught those worms yet? You can't stay out in the park alone all night."

"But Mom, I don't have enough worms to pay for Scooter's football. And I promised to get him a new one this week. I have one thousand one hundred and three worms and I need to catch one thousand three hundred and thirty-one altogether. I had some money saved and I earned some last night."

"Let's see. He needs two hundred and twenty-eight more. It shouldn't take long to catch them," Mr. Huggins said to Mrs. Huggins. "After all, he promised. Let's help him."

So Henry and his mother and father bent and pounced together. Henry felt a little uncomfortable to see his mother catching worms, but he was very, very glad when the one thousand three hundred and thirty-first worm was in the jar. He took his jars of worms to Mr. Grumbie, who paid him thirteen dollars and thirty-one cents. As Henry watched him turn the night crawlers into a box of dirt so they would live until Sunday, he thought he never wanted to see another worm.

He felt the money in his pocket. "I guess this ought to take care of old Scooter," he said and, wishing he could spend it on a football for him-

self, he went home to bed.

Sunday morning Henry lay on his stomach on the living-room floor reading the funny papers. Usually he woke up early and read the funnies before his mother and father were awake, but this morning he was so tired from catching worms that he slept later than usual.

The doorbell rang and Mr. Huggins, who was reading the sports section and drinking coffee, put down his paper and answered the door.

Henry heard a strange man ask, "Excuse me, could you tell me who owns this football?"

Henry didn't wait for his father to answer. He ran to the door.

The man was holding Scooter's real cowhide football, stitched with nylon thread and laced with buckskin thongs!

"Golly!" said Henry. "That's the football I lost for Scooter McCarthy."

The man handed it to Henry. "I'm sorry I couldn't stop when the ball landed in my car. I had to take my wife to the hospital in a hurry. I would have returned it sooner, but I couldn't leave the kids."

"That's O.K.," said Henry. "Gee, thanks for bringing it back."

When the man had gone, Henry showed the football to his father. "See, Dad," he said, "this is the kind of football I'm going to buy with my night crawler money." Then he tucked the football under his arm as if he were running ninety yards for a touchdown and sprinted down the street to Scooter's house.

CHAPTER FOUR

The Green Christmas

HENRY was glad he sat in the row by the windows in Room Four, because he could watch for snowflakes. Even though his father said they would probably have a green Christmas this year, Henry still hoped for snow. He was pretty sure the package hidden behind some boxes in the garage was the sled he wanted, a real Flexible Flyer.

While he sat at his desk looking out at the clouds for signs of snow, he was listening to Miss Roop talk about the Christmas operetta and thinking he had taken part in enough school plays for one semester.

In September he had been Second Indian in a play for the Westward Expansion Unit. That hadn't been too bad. He had stuck an old feather out of a duster in his hair and worn an auto robe his mother let him take to school. It was an easy part, because all he had to say was "Ugh!" First Indian and Third Indian also said "Ugh!" It really hadn't mattered which Indian said "Ugh!" Once all three said it at the same time.

Then in November Robert came down with mumps just before Book Week. At the last minute Henry had to wear a long cotton beard and read Robert's part, one of the seven dwarfs in a play called "Storyland Favorites Come to Life." It was not a play that appealed to Henry, but at least he did not have to memorize any lines or do much practicing, because there wasn't time. During the performance he had to stop reading several times in order to take pieces of his beard out of his mouth.

His worst part had been in a Parent Teacher program for National Brush Your Teeth Week. Henry had been really disgusted that day. He had to wear his best trousers and a white shirt to school and he had to stay clean all day. Then he missed practicing with his football, because the meeting was after school. Worst of all, he had to stand up in front of all the mothers and teachers, bow, and recite:

> I am Sir Cuspid,
> My job is to bite.
> Brush me twice daily
> To keep me so white.

The kids called him Sir Cuspidor for a long time after that.

Now Miss Roop was telling the class that the Christmas operetta was called "A Visit to Santa Claus." It was about a mother and father and their two children who visited Santa Claus at the North Pole on Christmas Eve. Henry thought it was a dumb play. In the end it turned out that the little boy had dreamed the whole thing. Henry disliked stories that ended by being someone's dream.

Miss Roop said, "Since the whole school is giving the operetta, there won't be parts for everyone in our room."

That's good, thought Henry. He slid way down in his seat so Miss Roop wouldn't notice him when she assigned parts.

Miss Roop continued. "Richard, Arthur, Ralph, and David will be four of Santa Claus's reindeer. The other four will be chosen from Room Five." So far Henry was safe! He stayed down in his seat just to be sure. "Mary Jane, you are to have the part of the Dancing Doll.

Beezus—uh, I mean Beatrice, you will be the Rag Doll." Girls' parts. Henry felt a little safer. "Robert, you will be the Big Brown Dog," Miss Roop went on. All the children laughed.

"Gr-r-r-r. Arf! Arf!" said Robert. The children laughed again.

When Miss Roop started to hand out the parts, Henry decided she had come to the end of the list. He sat up straight in his seat and looked out of the window at the sky. It looked darker. There might be snow before Christmas after all. He was glad he wouldn't have to stay in after school to rehearse "A Visit to Santa Claus." He wanted to make snow men and throw snowballs, since, of course, his mother and father would not give him the Flexible Flyer until Christmas. When he had his sled, he wanted to coast on the Thirty-third Street hill.

Miss Roop, holding one part in her hand, stood in front of the class again and smiled in Henry's direction. Just in case she was smiling at him, Henry quickly slid down in his seat again.

She *was* smiling at him. She said, "And the best part of all goes to Henry Huggins. Henry, you are the shortest boy in Room Four, so you are to have the part of Timmy, the little boy who dreams the whole story." The class shouted with laughter.

A little boy! It was worse than anything Henry had imagined. He could never live down the part of a little boy! Sir Cuspid had been bad enough, but a little boy—the kids would never stop teasing him. "Miss Roop," he said desperately, "there're lots of littler kids in the lower grades. Couldn't one of them have the part?"

"No, Henry. All the second and third grade boys are needed for the chorus of polar bears and the first grade boys are too little to learn so many lines." She handed Henry his part. So many carbons had been typed at one time that the thin paper was almost too blurry to read.

Henry made out:

ACT I. The scene is Timmy's bedroom. Timmy is wearing pajamas. Enter Timmy's mother.

TIMMY'S MOTHER: Hurry up and get into bed, Timmy. This is Christmas Eve and good little boys should be asleep when Santa Claus comes.

TIMMY: Yes, Mother. (Timmy gets into bed. His mother tucks him in and kisses him good night.)

TIMMY'S MOTHER: Good night, Timmy. Pleasant dreams. (Goes out and shuts door.)

TIMMY: Ho hum. My, I am sleepy! I wonder what Santa Claus will have for me in his pack. I think—I—will—try—to—stay—awake. (Falls asleep.)

Henry groaned. It was even worse than he had expected. Pajamas! Good-night kiss! Did they think he was going to stand up there on the stage in front of all the girls in the school in his pajamas? And be kissed by some dumb old eighth grade girl who was supposed to be his mother? It was horrible even to think about.

He had to find a way out! Already Robert was whispering across the aisle, "Hey, Little Boy!"

Henry ignored him. Maybe if he did stretching exercises for a whole hour every morning he would grow fast enough to outgrow the part.

No, that wouldn't work. There wasn't time. He would have to think of something else.

During the rest of the afternoon Henry had trouble keeping his mind on Social Studies. He was too busy trying to find a way out of playing Timmy, the Little Boy. When the last bell rang, he grabbed his beanie and raincoat from the cloakroom. He was first out of Room Four and first out of the school building.

Ribs was waiting under the fir tree out of the rain. "Come on, Ribsy," Henry yelled, "let's keep ahead of the rest of the kids!"

But he wasn't quite fast enough. Beezus and Robert and Scooter were right behind him. "Hi there, Timmy!" they yelled. "How's the Little Boy?" Then they began to chant, "Henry is a Little Boy! Henry is a Little Boy!"

Henry slowed down. "Aw, shut up!" he yelled back. "You think you're smart, but you're not. You're just an old Rag Doll and a Brown Dog. And I'll bet Scooter is something dumb, too!"

"You wouldn't catch me being in any old operetta," said Scooter loftily. "I'm on the stage crew. I get to pull the curtain and turn on the lights and paint the scenery and stuff."

Mary Jane came skipping down the street, jumping across the puddles on the sidewalk. "Here comes the old Dancing Doll!" yelled Henry.

"Yes." Mary Jane smiled proudly. "I'll wear my new ballet slippers and my pink taffeta party dress and have my hair curled."

The other children were disappointed. They couldn't tease Mary Jane if she wanted to be a Dancing Doll. It gave Henry an idea. He waited until Scooter said, "I'll bet the Little Boy will look real cute in his pajamas. Are you going to wear the kind with feet in them, Little Boy?"

"Aw, you're just jealous because you don't have an important part like I have. I have the most important part in the whole operetta!"

"Don't be funny!" Scooter laughed. "I wouldn't

learn all those lines and run around in front of a bunch of people in my pajamas for a million trillion dollars!"

It was a good idea but it didn't work. Henry would have to think of something else. Maybe he could pretend to be sick. No, that wouldn't do. His mother would make him go to bed and if it did happen to snow, he would have to stay in the house while all the other children were out sliding on the Thirty-third Street hill.

By the time Henry reached his house on Klickitat Street, he decided to say nothing about the operetta to his mother and father until he could work things out. He said hello to his mother, who was writing a letter on the typewriter, and then he went into the kitchen to fix himself a snack of peanut butter, jam, and pickle relish on graham crackers. He spread a cracker with peanut butter and gave it to Ribsy. Then he leaned against the refrigerator to munch and think.

Tap-tap-tap went the typewriter. Henry fixed

himself another cracker. Tap-tap-tap. He heard his mother pull the sheet of paper out of the machine. Then he heard her go into the bedroom. The typewriter—that was it!

"Hey, Mom, can I use the typewriter?"

"*May* I use the typewriter."

"May I use the typewriter?" asked Henry patiently.

"Yes, Henry, but don't pound too hard."

Henry gulped down his graham cracker with peanut butter, jam, and pickle relish. He wiped his fingers on the seat of his jeans and went into the living room. There he sat down at the desk, took a sheet of paper from the drawer, and put it into the typewriter. He thought a while and then began to type. He didn't make the typewriter go tap-tap-tap the way his mother did. He made only one tap at a time and then, after a long pause while he looked for the right letter, he made another tap. He had to remind himself to push the extra key to make capital letters.

Henry worked a long time. Fortunately his mother did not pay any attention to his typing. Tap. Tap. Tap. At last it was finished. Henry pulled the paper out of the typewriter and read:

dEar mIss rrOOP?
P½easee xcuze henry from the ~~oppar~~ ~~o̸p̸ȧ̸r̸t̸~~ Play/HE Has to mucj workk todo at homeȼ.
                    yYourz turly.
                    MRs, hUggins

Somehow it didn't look the way he had thought it would. The capitals were not in the right places. He knew *much* wasn't spelled with a *j* or *yours* with a *z*. His fingers had just put themselves on the wrong keys. Henry tore his letter into little pieces and threw them in the fireplace. He ran another piece of paper into the typewriter and started again. Tap. Tap. Tap. When the second letter was finished, it read:

DEar misS rOop.
P PLease ezcude Henry Fro m the play? eH has *tw̸o̸* too much wwork to̸ doat home.
                    YYours turly/
                    mRs, hUggins

Henry studied it. Those capitals again. He pushed the thing too soon or not soon enough. And who ever heard of a word like *ezcude?* Or *doat?* His fingers just didn't hit the right keys. No, the letter was not a finished product. Henry tore this one up, too, and threw it in the fireplace. He would have to think of something else.

When rehearsals started after school the next day, Henry still had not thought of a way out.

Miss Roop said that today the children would read their parts, but by next week they must have them memorized. "Henry, you and Alice are on the stage first," she directed. Alice was the eighth grade girl who was to play the part of Timmy's mother. "Come on, Henry, don't waste time."

Henry slouched up the steps to the stage. He pulled his crumpled part out of his hip pocket and looked at it. He decided to pretend he couldn't read it. Maybe if he read everything wrong, Miss Roop would give someone else the part.

Alice read, "Hurry up and get into bed, Timmy. This is Christmas Eve and good little boys should be asleep when Santa Claus comes."

Henry held the paper almost against his nose. He frowned and squinted. He didn't say, "Yes, Mother." He said, after scowling and twisting the paper around, "Yeah, Ma."

"Henry Huggins!" Miss Roop interrupted. "You read what is typed on that paper!"

"Well, gee whiz, Miss Roop, it's so blurry I can hardly see what it says."

"Bring your part to me."

Henry slouched off the stage and handed it to her. "Now Henry, it isn't as blurred as all that. However, since you have such a long part you had better trade with me."

Well, that's that, thought Henry. None of his ideas seemed to work.

"Continue," ordered Miss Roop.

The operetta proceeded. It seemed to Henry that it took a long time to go through it. The music teacher played the music for the songs they were supposed to learn by next week. Henry discovered that in the second act he was supposed to stand in the center of the stage and sing a song all by himself. It went:

> Hurrah for Santa! Hurrah for Saint Nick!
> He comes from the North with reindeer and sleigh,
> Riding on clouds up high in the sky
> With a pack full of toys so children can play.

It was the dumbest song Henry had ever heard. Hurrah for Santa! It was just plain stupid. He felt a little better when he learned that Robert had to sing an even dumber song called "Woof, Woof, I'm a Big Brown Dog."

As Christmas drew near, Henry became more and more discouraged. Everybody in Glenwood School called him Little Boy. His mother and father found out about his part in the play, because Mary Jane told her mother and she told Henry's mother. He had to learn his lines and recite them every evening while his father looked at the part and prompted him. He scarcely had time to go out to the garage to peek at the Flexible Flyer package.

Mrs. Huggins went downtown to buy him a pair of new pajamas to wear in the first act. They were made of pink-and-blue-and-white-striped flannel. Henry felt that any pajamas were bad enough—but pink-and-blue pajamas! He didn't even like to think about them.

Henry swallowed hard every morning. He hoped his throat might be a little bit sore but it never was. Finally he gave up. There was no way out. Now all he wanted was to get it over.

One afternoon during fifth period Henry looked out of the window and saw a few feathery snowflakes drifting down. They were so light he wasn't sure at first. When Miss Roop wasn't looking, he leaned over closer to the window. It was snow, all right! It wasn't going to be a green Christmas after all! Now he would get to use his Flexible Flyer!

The rest of the class soon noticed the snow too, and everyone began to whisper. Miss Roop smiled and pretended not to hear. As soon as the bell rang, the children all scrambled for their wraps and rushed out to see the snow—all except those who had parts in the operetta. They took their wraps from the cloakroom and went to the auditorium.

The auditorium was a busy place. In one corner of the room, mothers from the Parent Teacher Association were altering costumes for the polar bear chorus. Henry remembered those white suits. He had worn one when he had been an Easter bunny in a spring program. Now the mothers were ripping off the long ears and fuzzy tails, and were sewing on short ears and straight tails to change the suits into polar bear costumes.

The stage crew was at work. Some of the eighth grade boys were turning different-colored lights on and off. At the back of the stage, Scooter, standing on a board laid across two stepladders, was painting scenery with green paint.

Henry sat down to wait for his turn, while Mary Jane and Beezus rehearsed their dance, and Robert, wearing his dog suit, practiced walking on all fours.

Henry waited and waited. He sat on the hard auditorium chair and looked out of the window at the snowflakes. He could hear the other kids laughing and yelling outside, so he knew there must be enough snow for snowballs. He wished his turn would come so he could leave. Now the tin soldiers were practicing their steps. At the end of their song and dance one of the stage crew threw a basketball across the stage in front of them. It was supposed to look like a cannon ball, and the tin soldiers were supposed to fall over with one leg in the air. Miss Roop didn't like the way they fell and she made them do it over several times.

Henry wandered up on the stage behind the tin soldiers to watch Scooter paint scenery. "What're you supposed to be painting?" he asked him.

"Trees," answered Scooter. "With real paint."

"Where did you get it?"

"A fellow in my room's father has a paint store and he gave it to us."

Just then Henry heard a bark. It sounded like Ribsy. It *was* Ribsy. He bounded in through the door of the auditorium, ran up the steps to the stage, and wormed his way behind the row of tin soldiers to get to Henry. He shook himself and wagged his tail.

"Well, Ribsy, old boy!" said Henry. "Did you get tired of waiting out in the cold?" Ribsy shook himself again. Henry patted him. "Why, Ribs, you're all wet! It must be snowing hard."

"He's a dumb-looking dog," said Scooter.

"Aw, he is not. He's a smart dog. Aren't you, Ribsy?"

"I'll bet he can't climb a stepladder like my dog can," said Scooter.

"I'll bet he can. Call him and see."

Scooter looked down at the dog. "Here, Ribsy," he called. "Come on, boy." Ribsy looked at him and then at Henry.

"Go on," said Henry. "Up the ladder." He pointed to the ladder. Ribsy put one paw on the bottom step. "Atta boy, go on!" Ribsy carefully put a paw on the next step. "Good dog!" said Henry, urging him on.

"Come on, Ribsy," coaxed Scooter. Ribsy cautiously made his way up to the board on top of the stepladders.

"Good old Ribsy!" said Henry. "See, I told you he could do it!"

Pleased with himself, Ribsy looked down at his master, wagged his tail, and said, "Woof!"

"You be quiet!" ordered Henry in a loud

whisper. "If Miss Roop hears you, she'll throw you out!"

Ribsy sat down on the board and looked around the auditorium.

"Beat it!" said Scooter. "Can't you see I have work to do?"

"Here, Ribsy!" whispered Henry. "You don't want Miss Roop to see you, do you?"

Ribsy liked sitting on the board.

"See, I told you he was a dumb dog." Scooter picked up his can of paint and stepped over Ribsy. He set the can down and went on painting treetops.

"Come on, Ribsy!"

"Aw, he's too dumb to go down the ladder."

"He is not! Here, Ribsy!"

Ribsy stood up and sniffed at the can of paint. "Here, Ribsy! Come on down," begged Henry, looking up at his dog. "Come on, you old dog. I'll catch it if Miss Roop sees you."

Miss Roop clapped her hands for attention,

the music ceased, and the tin soldiers stopped falling down.

"How did that dog get in here?" she demanded.

"I don't know," answered Henry. "I guess he just walked in."

"Well, take him out!"

Henry did not move.

"Quickly, Henry! We have a lot to do this afternoon."

"Gee whiz, Miss Roop, I'm trying to take him out but he won't come down."

"I'll carry him down, Miss Roop," offered Scooter. "I don't think he knows how to go down a ladder."

Henry glared at Scooter.

"No, he's too heavy to carry down a ladder. You might fall," said Miss Roop.

Just then Ribsy sat down to scratch behind his left ear. Thump. Thump. Thump. His hind leg bumped against the can of paint. The can tipped. Scooter yelled. Ribsy barked.

"Henry! Look out!" screamed Miss Roop.

The can fell over and green paint poured down over Henry.

"Glub!" said Henry as he heard Miss Roop run up onto the stage. He heard her but he couldn't see her. He had to keep his eyes shut. The cold, oily paint was dribbling down his face and neck. He could feel it dripping off his ears.

Miss Roop made a squeaking noise. Then Henry could feel her rubbing his head with something made of cloth.

"Run and get some paper towels!" she called to the other children. She wiped away at his face. "I knew I shouldn't have let those boys use real paint. They should have used poster paint. It would have washed off. Oh dear, I'm afraid your shirt is ruined."

Henry heard Ribsy barking. When he could see again he found all the tin soldiers and polar bears and P.T.A. mothers crowded around him. Miss Roop began to scrub his hair with paper towels. "Oh, that's all right," he said to Miss Roop. "It's an old shirt anyway." The towels she was wiping him with felt scratchy on his ears and neck.

Ribsy continued to bark and to pace back and forth across the board as he looked down at his master.

"Quiet, Ribsy!" ordered Henry.

Ribsy stopped barking and looked anxiously at the floor. Then he looked at Henry. Before Henry realized what was happening, Ribsy leaped from the board, sailed over the heads of several tin soldiers and polar bears, and landed on all fours in the puddle of paint. He skidded and sat down.

"Ribsy!" groaned Henry. Then he said to Scooter, "See, he was smart enough to get down by himself."

The dog began to bark and run around Henry. He left a circle of green footprints on the floor of the stage.

"Oh, Henry," wailed Miss Roop and then said sharply, "Scooter, take that dog out of the building! And carry him. I don't want any green footprints in the halls!"

"Yes, Miss Roop." Scooter lugged the barking dog away.

Mary Jane squirmed through the crowd to look at Henry. "Henry Huggins!" she exclaimed. "Wait till your mother sees you! Your hair is green and so is your skin!"

Beezus laughed. "Henry, your face looks just like a green apple!"

"Henry, I'm afraid this isn't going to come off for a long time," said Miss Roop.

Someone handed Henry a mirror. "Golly!" breathed Henry. He stared into the mirror. His hair and eyebrows were pale green. His face was all green at the forehead and streaked with green toward his chin. His ears were green all over. "Jeepers! Green ears!" He couldn't take his eyes off the mirror. Secretly he thought he looked fascinating. Like a leprechaun in a fairy tale. Now maybe the kids would stop calling him Little Boy! That gave him an idea.

"Miss Roop, I can't be in the operetta when I'm all green, can I?" he asked hopefully.

Miss Roop sighed. "No, Henry, I guess you can't." She looked at him. Then she smiled. "I'll give your part to someone else and you can play the part of the Green Elf! Now run along home."

The Green Elf! That was a good part. The Green Elf turned somersaults and didn't have to say anything.

Henry put on his raincoat and beanie and went out into the snow. It was deep enough to scrunch under his feet. He scooped up a handful and threw it at Ribsy, who was waiting under the fir tree. The snow would be just right for coasting on the Thirty-third Street hill when his mother and father surprised him with the Flexible Flyer at Christmas. In the meantime he would make a snow man on the front lawn. Maybe he would make a whole snow family. Even a snow dog.

"Good old Ribsy. I don't know how I'd ever get along without you." He took out his handkerchief and wiped green paint from his dog's tail.

Then Henry followed a set of big footprints in the snow. He took big steps and carefully put his feet into the marks someone else had made in the snow. "Jeepers!" he exclaimed. "I'm going to have a green Christmas and a white Christmas at the same time. Won't Mom be surprised?"

CHAPTER FIVE

The Pale Pink Dog

WHEN Henry woke up one Monday morning in the spring, the first thing he thought was, Five more days till Saturday. On Tuesday the first thing he thought was, Four more days till Saturday. By Wednesday he felt as if Saturday would never come.

It all began when Henry and Ribsy made their weekly trip to the Lucky Dog Pet Shop to buy horse meat.

"Well, if it isn't Henry and Ribs!" exclaimed Mr. Pennycuff. "Do you have your entry blank for the dog show?"

"What dog show?" asked Henry.

"Didn't you hear? The park department is having a dog show in the park next Saturday. Boys and girls up to sixteen years old may enter their dogs. The Woofies Dog Food Company is giving prizes. Better take an entry blank and fill it out. A fine dog like Ribsy is sure to win a prize."

Ribsy wagged his tail.

"Well," said Henry doubtfully, "he's an awfully good dog but he isn't any special kind. I mean he isn't a cocker or bulldog or anything."

"That doesn't matter in this show. Now you just take this blank and fill it out. See, here's a place for dogs of mixed breed like Ribs."

"Gee, thanks," said Henry. "I think I will."

He took his entry blank and two pounds of horse meat, and he and Ribsy ran all the way home.

When they came to Klickitat Street, Henry saw Scooter and Robert playing catch. Mary Jane and Beezus and her little sister Ramona were standing under a snowball bush, shaking

petals down over themselves and pretending it
was snowing.

"Hey, look!" yelled Henry, waving the paper
at them.

The children gathered around him to look at his
entry blank. "I'm going to enter Ribsy," said
Henry. "He'll win a prize. Mr. Pennycuff said so."

"Aw, Ribsy's just an old mutt!" scoffed Scooter.

"He is not! He's a smart dog and besides, it
says he doesn't have to be any special kind of
dog. See, it says dogs of mixed breed."

"Say, look at the list of prizes!" said Robert.
"Woofies Dog Food, squeaking mice, feeding
dishes, leashes, movie tickets, beanies, silver
loving cups—a whole lot of stuff."

"If they're giving silver cups, I'm going to get a blank for Princess Patricia of Tarabrook. She's a better dog than Ribsy," said Mary Jane.

"Princess who?" demanded Scooter.

"Princess Patricia of Tarabrook. That's Patsy's real name. She has a pedigree and I know she'll win a silver cup." Patsy was Mary Jane's cocker spaniel.

"You know," said Robert thoughtfully, "I'm going to enter Sassy. She's getting kind of old, but she's still pretty lively and she might win a movie ticket or something."

Beezus and Ramona didn't have a dog. They had a cat, three white rats, a turtle, and one guppy. Beezus said she knew where she could borrow a puppy named Puddles.

"Well, I guess I might as well enter Rags," said Scooter. "He's the smartest dog around here. He can even sit up and shake hands. And he's all Airedale, too. He isn't any mixed breed like that old mutt you found."

"Ribsy isn't old and he isn't a mutt either! And he can sit up, too. He's a better dog than your old Rags and he'll win a better prize. I'll bet he wins a silver cup!"

"Don't make me laugh!" scoffed Scooter. "If he'd been any good, his folks wouldn't have let him get away."

At last Saturday came. Henry jumped out of bed as soon as he woke up, because he had a lot to do before the dog show at ten o'clock. At breakfast he stopped gulping his cereal to ask, "Mom, can I give Ribsy a bath in the bathtub?"

"*May* I give Ribsy a bath in the bathtub."

"May I give Ribsy a bath in the bathtub?"

"Can't you use the laundry tub in the basement the way you usually do?" his mother asked.

"But, Mom, this is special for the dog show. I want to do an extra good job on him this time. If I get him good and clean, I know he'll win a silver cup."

Mrs. Huggins sighed. "Yes, Henry, you may

give Ribsy a bath in the bathtub if you'll promise to clean up the bathroom afterward."

"Thanks, Mom. I'll clean it up. Excuse me, please."

"Henry, I'm afraid you didn't eat much breakfast. I hope Ribsy does win a silver cup, but I wouldn't count on it too much if I were you. After all, he's just a mongrel."

"He isn't a mongrel, Mom. He's a mixed breed. And I know he's a better dog than any dog around here. Come on, Ribsy."

Ribsy followed Henry into the bathroom. When Henry began to run the water into the tub, he looked at Henry and then at the water. Then he tucked his tail between his legs and started to sneak out of the bathroom.

"Oh no you don't!" Henry grabbed him by the collar. He put his arms around Ribsy's middle and lifted him into the tub. Ribsy was heavier than he had been that day about a year ago when Henry carried him into the bus.

Because this was a special occasion, Henry didn't use flea soap. He used his mother's shampoo. Ribsy whimpered. Henry rubbed the shampoo on him and worked it into a thick lather. He rubbed and scrubbed. The suds foamed thick and white until Ribsy, except for his face, was hidden in mounds of thick lather.

"Now you ought to be good and clean," said Henry. He scooped up handfuls of water from the tub and poured them over the dog. He poured and poured but the lather only grew thicker. If only he hadn't used so much shampoo! He tried mopping Ribsy with his washcloth. That helped but it still wasn't fast enough. He had an idea. He moved Ribsy around so that he faced the end of the tub, and turned the shower on him. Ribsy tried to jump out but Henry held him. Ribsy raised his head and howled.

"Henry!" his mother called. "What are you doing to that poor dog?"

"Just washing him," answered Henry, and

turned off the shower. Ribsy shook himself. Henry used four bath towels on him, but still he wasn't dry.

Oh well, it's a warm day. Maybe the sun will dry him off, thought Henry. He took one of the towels and hastily wiped it over the floor and tub.

"Henry, I have to go downtown this morning. I hope you and Ribsy have good luck at the dog show." Mrs. Huggins had her hat on, ready to leave.

"Thanks, Mom. Say, have you seen the leash? It says on the entry blank all dogs must be on a leash."

"I think you left it in the basement," Mrs. Huggins said as she went out.

Henry ran down to the basement. At the bottom of the stairs he found the leash—at least, it had been a leash once. Now it was chewed into half a dozen pieces. Henry looked hurriedly around for something to use in its place. If only he had more time! The only thing he could find was his mother's rainy day clothesline. After climbing up on an apple box to untie it, he ran upstairs and fastened one end to Ribsy's collar. It was longer than a leash but it would have to do.

When Henry went out on the front porch, he saw Beezus and Ramona coming down the street. Beezus was carrying a squirming black puppy that kept trying to lick her face. "Puddles, you stop that!" she commanded and set him on the sidewalk. Puddles was wearing a red bow on his collar and Henry was pleased to see that Ribsy wasn't the only dog with a rope for a leash.

"Come on, Henry, we'd better hurry," said Beezus.

Ribsy sniffed at the puppy and decided to ignore him. "Hey, look," exclaimed Henry. "There's Mary Jane and Patsy and Robert and Sassy up there ahead. We'd better run."

When they reached the park, Henry saw that already there were hundreds of boys and girls and dogs there ahead of them. Henry had never seen so many dogs. There were boxers, Great Danes, Pekingese, Airedales, cockers, Saint Bernards, Pomeranians, beagles, setters, pointers, and just plain dogs. Some, like Puddles, were wearing ribbons on their collars, some wore sweaters, and some had on little paper hats.

A loud-speaker on a sound truck blared out. "Take your entry blanks to the registration desk by the tennis courts."

"Come on, Ribsy." Henry found his way through the crowds of children and dogs to the registration desk. There he waited in line to weigh Ribsy on a big scale. At first Ribsy didn't want to be weighed, but Henry and a boy scout managed to shove him upon the scale and keep him still long enough to see that he weighed twenty-eight pounds.

"You've grown a lot heavier in a year," said Henry. "Maybe we shouldn't call you Ribsy any more."

After the dog was weighed, a lady gave Henry a yellow cardboard arm band. It had "Woofies Dog Food—Woofies make dogs woof for joy" printed on it. Below that there was a space for the kind of dog, weight-class, and the ring in which the dog was to be shown. The lady wrote on it, "Mixed breed—25 to 40 pounds—Ring 3."

Henry led Ribsy toward a sign with "Ring 3"

printed on it over by a flower bed. Ribsy stopped to shake himself and then, before Henry knew what was happening, he dashed over to the flower bed and rolled in the dirt.

"Hey, cut that out!" yelled Henry. "You're getting all dirty."

It was too late. Henry pulled Ribsy, streaked with mud, out of the flowers. Henry tried to brush off the dirt. Then he tried to rub it off with his handkerchief. He only smeared it. He was discouraged. Why had he bragged so much about his dog? Now he would never win a prize.

When Henry reached Ring 3, he saw that it was made of rope tied to four stakes driven into the ground. Inside was a table piled with the prizes Henry had read about. Henry looked at the silver cup and thought it would look nice on his dresser. Not that he had a chance with a muddy dog. He noticed some of the boys had brought brushes and were brushing their dogs. He wished he had thought to bring a brush.

The day was warm. Henry sat down on the grass with the rest of the boys and girls to wait for the judging to start. He kept trying to brush some of the dirt off Ribsy. In the ring next to his he saw a snow-white dog. Somebody said it was a Siberian sled dog. The dog's owner was brushing him and sprinkling white powder on him to make him look whiter.

Henry had an idea! If he only had time, he could run home for a can of talcum powder to sprinkle on the white parts of Ribsy! That would cover up the dirt. It didn't matter about the yellow and black and brown parts. The dirt didn't show there much.

Just then the voice boomed over the loud-speaker. "We are going to postpone the judging for a little while, because we have a real treat for all you kids. Maud, the trained mule, is going to entertain you."

The children all started toward the truck to see Maud. That is, all except Henry. He was not interested in any trained mule. He wanted Ribsy to win a silver cup. Here was his chance. He could run home and back while Maud the mule performed.

"Come on, Ribsy!" he yelled. "We have to step on it."

Followed by Ribsy, he ran as fast as he could out of the park and up the hill to his house on Klickitat Street. He rushed into his room and snatched his hairbrush. He tore into the bathroom and grabbed a can of talcum powder. Then he rushed back to the park with Ribsy. The children were still crowded around Maud.

Henry was so hot and sticky that he had to sit

down on the grass to catch his breath. Ribsy was panting and his tongue hung out. Henry brushed him with the hairbrush. That helped a little. Then he sprinkled powder on the big white spot on his back.

Henry was horrified. He could scarcely believe what he saw. The talcum powder wasn't white—it was pink! Who ever heard of a dog with pink spots! Quickly he tried to brush the powder off. But Ribsy was still damp and the powder didn't brush off.

Henry decided to make all Ribsy's white parts pink so they would match. Maybe in the bright sunshine the judges wouldn't notice. He sprinkled powder on Ribsy's white ear and left hind paw. He even sprinkled some on his white tail. Yes, Ribsy did look better with all his light parts matching. Maybe the judges would wear dark glasses.

Maud finished her act and the children came back to the rings with their dogs. "Hey, look at the pink dog!" a boy exclaimed.

"I never heard of a pink dog," a girl said. "What kind is he?"

"He's a mixed breed," said Henry.

He put the talcum powder can in his pocket and decided not to say anything about it. Maybe the others would think he had some rare breed of dog.

A man stood in the center of the ring. Henry noticed that he was not wearing dark glasses. "All right," the man called. "Bring your dogs into the ring and march them around in single file."

"Come on, Ribsy, they're going to start judging. You'd better behave yourself." Henry led him by the clothesline into the ring.

The children walked their dogs around in a circle. Ribsy's long rope tangled with the other dogs' leashes. Finally the judge directed them to stop. "Now get your dogs ready," he ordered.

Henry didn't know what he meant, so he watched the others. Some of them knelt by their dogs and made them stand still and look ahead.

That must be what the judge meant. Henry knelt beside Ribsy. Ribsy sat down. He opened his mouth and let his long pink tongue hang out. He was thirsty.

"Come on, Ribs, stand up," begged Henry. "Be a good dog." Ribsy began to pant. "Come on, get up!"

Ribsy lay down on the grass and panted harder. Henry pulled and tugged. He looked over his shoulder at the judge. The judge was looking at the ears and teeth of a dog that was standing properly. Then he ran his hands over the dog. The dog didn't move.

"Come on, Ribsy!" begged Henry. "It'll be our turn pretty soon." Ribsy closed his eyes. "I know you're thirsty. I'll get you a drink of water just as soon as I can."

The loud-speaker made an announcement. "Will the boy scouts please take pans of water to each ring?"

Henry was relieved to see a boy scout coming

with water, but when Ribsy's turn came, he sniffed at the pan and refused to drink.

"I guess he's used to his own dishes," explained Henry. "He just doesn't want to use the same pan as the other dogs."

"Can't help it," said the boy scout. "It's the only one I have."

Ribsy continued to pant.

At last the judge came to Henry. "Well, well, a pink dog," he exclaimed.

"Yes, sir," said Henry. It was lucky his own green hair had grown out so it could be cut off. A green-haired boy and a pale-pink dog would have looked funny.

"Come on, son. Stand him up."

Henry boosted Ribsy to his feet. Ribsy tried to sit down again, but Henry held up his hind end by the tail. The judge looked at his ears and teeth. Then he ran his hands over him. He looked at his fingers afterward. They were pink. "Hmmmm," he said.

When the judge had looked at all the dogs, he ordered each child to walk across the ring and back with his dog. Henry noticed that the boys and girls who knew about these things held the leash in the left hand. When his turn came he held the clothesline in his left hand and started across the ring. Halfway across, Ribsy sat down to scratch behind his left ear. Henry pulled at the rope. When he reached the other side of the ring and turned back, Ribsy turned the wrong way so that he crossed in front of Henry.

Henry tripped on the rope and started to change it to his right hand, but just then Ribsy ran around behind Henry to growl at a dog that was mostly spaniel. The boy who owned the spaniel pulled him away and started to the other side of the ring. Ribsy ran in front of Henry and pulled at his rope to get closer to the other dog. The harder he pulled, the tighter the rope drew around Henry's legs. The children began to laugh. Ribsy was so excited he ran around behind Henry and pulled the rope even tighter. The laughter increased.

"Cut that out, Ribsy!" Henry ordered, looking over his shoulder at his dog. He felt silly standing there wound up in a clothesline.

"Come on, son," said the judge. "We can't waste time. A lot of other boys and girls want to show their dogs, too."

Now, on top of all his troubles, the judge was cross with him. Henry knew a cross judge would never give him a silver cup. Discouraged and feeling even sillier, Henry twirled around like a top to unwind himself from the rope. Relieved to have that part of the show over, he dragged Ribsy to the side of the ring. In a few minutes he could take his dog home and give him a drink.

After each child had walked his dog, the judge went around the ring pointing to different boys and girls, saying, "All right, you stay in the ring." He looked at Henry and his dog. "Hmmmm," he said. "All right, you stay in."

As the contestants left the ring, the boy scouts

handed them prizes. Those who left first won the smallest prizes. The longer they stayed in the ring, the bigger the prize.

"Hey, Henry, are you still in?" Henry looked up. Robert and Sassy were standing outside the rope.

"Yes," answered Henry, "and I sure don't see why. Ribsy did everything wrong. Did Sassy win anything?"

"Just a dog whistle." Robert took another look at Ribsy. "Say, how did he get all pink?"

"Aw, mind your own beeswax," said Henry. He pretended to be watching the judge carefully. One by one the man asked the boys and girls to leave the ring.

"Look what I won!" Henry saw Beezus waving a rubber mouse. "See, it squeaks!" She squeaked it. Then she stopped. "Look!" she squealed. "Ribsy is pink!"

"Shut up!" Henry looked at the judge. He wished he knew why he was staying in the ring.

Every time the judge passed him he looked at Ribsy and said, "Hmmmm. Stay in the ring."

Mary Jane was the next one to see him. "See, I won a pillow for Patsy to sleep on," she said and then looked at Ribsy. "Why, Henry Huggins! What did you do to that poor dog? He's all pink. Just wait till your mother finds out about this."

"You keep quiet!" Henry said fiercely. There were only a few left in the ring.

Scooter was last to arrive. "Hi, Henry," he said. "Are you and that old mutt still in the ring? The judge must be blind. I guess Rags is a pretty good dog. Just the best in his class is all, and now he has to go to another ring to compete for the best dog in the show." He held up a small silver cup. Like the others, he looked at Ribsy. "I must be seeing things! A pink dog!" Scooter began to laugh. He sat down on the grass, laughing so hard he rolled back and forth.

Henry didn't think Ribsy was that funny. By this time Henry was so hot and disgusted that all he wanted was to get out of the ring, go home and get Ribsy a drink of water out of his own private pan.

"Hmmmm," said the judge again. At last only Henry and another boy were left. Henry remembered that the other boy's dog had done all the right things.

The judge stepped to the center of the ring with a silver cup in his hand. Henry wasn't at all surprised when the judge handed it to the other boy. He just wondered why he hadn't been asked to leave the ring. He thought he must have made a mistake, but the judge said to Henry and the winner, "Come along to the main ring. There will be some more judging there."

Puzzled, Henry followed. Beezus and Ramona, Scooter, Mary Jane, and Robert, and their dogs followed Henry. Maybe Henry was going to win a prize after all.

In the main ring were the prize winners from all the other rings. Henry noticed two big silver

cups on the table and saw his judge whispering
to the other judges. They all looked at Ribsy.
Ribsy panted harder than ever. The judges had
the winners show their dogs again.

This time Henry wasn't taking any chances with the clothesline getting wound around his legs. He wound it around his hand so that there was only a foot of rope between his hand and Ribsy's collar. Ribsy did not behave any better the second time he was shown than he had the first. When Henry's turn came to lead him across the ring, he stopped to growl at a boxer. The boxer growled back.

Henry heard Scooter say, "If that mutt doesn't look out, he's going to get all bit up."

Ribsy growled louder. The snarling boxer advanced, dragging the little girl who owned him along on the end of his leash.

Henry tried to pull Ribsy away but Ribsy ignored him. The dogs circled around one another, pulling their owners after them. Henry yanked so hard at Ribsy's collar the dog choked. The boxer snarled and sprang at Ribsy, using his powerful front paws to knock over the smaller dog. Henry's hand was wound in the rope and he could not let go. He was pulled down on his stomach with his face in the grass.

"Look! Henry's in a dog fight!" screamed Beezus in great excitement.

The boxer's owner began to cry.

Henry was so mixed up he wasn't sure what was happening. He smelled the damp grass and felt it tickling his nose. He could hear snarls, growls, and barks. He could hear children screaming and yelling. The boxer stepped on his back. Henry said, "Oof!" He lifted his face from the grass in time to see a boy scout try to stop the fight by throwing a pan of water at the dogs. He missed the dogs but he didn't miss Henry.

Two judges ran into the ring and grabbed the dogs by their hind legs. They yanked the snarling animals apart.

"All right, son. Go ahead," ordered one judge, while the other helped the little girl hold her boxer.

Embarrassed and dripping, Henry got up from

the grass and, without looking either right or left, hurried Ribsy across the ring and back.

Finally only Henry and another boy were left. The judge stepped to the center of the ring. "The big cup for the best dog in the whole show goes to the boy with the setter." Everybody clapped when he handed the boy one of the big silver cups. Ribsy growled at the winner.

"And now," said the judge, "the cup for the most unusual dog in the show goes to the boy with the a—a—mixed-breed dog!" He handed Henry the other big silver cup.

"Gee, thanks," was all Henry could say. The audience clapped and he heard Beezus shout, "Hooray for Henry!" He thought Ribsy looked pleased.

Everyone gathered around to admire his cup until a newspaper photographer asked them to stand back while he took a picture of Henry and his dog and wrote down his name and address. Henry was going to have his picture in the paper!

"Congratulations," said Scooter, "but I still think he's a mutt."

"Well, anyway, he won a bigger cup than Rags," boasted Henry, "but I guess Rags is a pretty good dog, too. Good old Ribsy. Now we'll get you a drink of water."

He led Ribsy to the nearest drinking fountain. He filled the silver cup with water and put it on the ground. Ribsy greedily lapped the water. Henry patted him. "Good old Ribsy. I knew you wouldn't drink out of any dish but your own."

———

CHAPTER SIX

Finders Keepers

AFTER lunch on the Saturday after the dog show Henry was in his room feeding his catfish. He dropped a tiny pinch of food into the water and watched it drift down to the bottom of the aquarium, where the catfish busily dug through the sand to find it.

"He-e-e-nry!" Robert was calling from the front yard.

Henry put the lid back on his aquarium and went out on the front porch. "Hi. What do you want?"

"Come on out and let's practice tumbling like the fellows in the gym at the Y."

"O.K." Henry ran down the front steps. Ribsy looked up from the bone he was gnawing and growled. It was not a cross growl. It was a growl that meant, "Don't bother me. Can't you see I'm busy?"

The boys practiced standing on their hands and turning somersaults on the lawn until Robert said, "Come on, let's try that trick where one fellow gets on his back with his feet in the air and the other fellow gets on top of his feet and the first fellow turns him around and around." He flopped on the grass with his feet in the air. "Come on. Try it," he said.

Henry sat on Robert's feet and lay back with his arms and legs outstretched. Robert tried to twirl him around. Henry teetered.

"Hey, you're kicking me!" Henry toppled over upon Robert.

"Oof!" Robert sat up. "You're too heavy. Let's try something else."

"I know what. Let's go over to Beezus' house

and practice chinning ourselves on her chestnut tree."

They found the girls in front of Beezus' house. They were busy tying a long jumping rope from the horse chestnut tree across the sidewalk to the lilac bush. Ramona, who was wearing pink coveralls and curlers in her hair, was scratching on the bark of the chestnut tree with her fingernails.

"Hi," said Henry.

"Hello," answered Beezus, stopping work on the rope.

"Mewow, mewow," said Ramona.

"What does she mean, 'Mewow'?" asked Henry.

"Oh, don't pay any attention to her," answered Beezus. "That's the way she says miaow. She's pretending she's a cat."

"Mewow," said Ramona and patted the curlers in her hair. "I'm a cat with curly hair."

Henry and Robert exchanged disgusted looks. Girls certainly started to be dumb when they were awfully young. They watched the girls in silence. Then they all sat down on the grass and waited.

"I wish you'd go away," said Mary Jane at last. "We're busy."

"Don't mind us," said Henry. "We have all day."

Beezus tightened the knot on the jumping rope. "Henry Huggins! I think you're mean. Why don't you play in your own yard?"

"We want to watch what you're doing," answered Henry, chewing on a blade of grass.

"Ho! I know. I'll bet you think you're going to be tight-rope walkers!" scoffed Robert. "Why don't you tie the rope up high? It's only about two feet off the ground."

"Dumbbell!" said Beezus. "Every time we walk across it without falling off we'll move it up a foot. I'll bet even people in circuses don't start practicing at the top of the circus tent. And they have nets under them, too."

"Aw, you can't even walk it when it's two feet off the ground," scoffed Henry. "I'll bet you couldn't walk it if it were one inch off the ground."

"You be quiet, Henry Huggins!" ordered Mary Jane. "Why don't you and Robert mind your own business? Go on, Beezus. Let's not pay any attention to them. They just think they're smart."

Beezus opened her mother's umbrella and held it in her right hand. As she stepped up on the rope, Mary Jane took hold of her left hand to steady her. The lilac bush bent under her weight, the rope sagged, and Beezus was standing on the sidewalk with the rope under her feet.

Robert and Henry hooted with laughter. "You sure look silly standing there on that rope with that umbrella in your hand!"

"You keep quiet!" snapped Beezus. "Let's see you do it if you think you're so smart."

Henry laughed harder. "She can't even walk it when it's a trillionth of an inch off the sidewalk!"

Robert rolled on the grass. "Not even if it's a billionth of a trillionth of an inch off the sidewalk!"

Beezus waved the umbrella. "You get off my property!"

"You can't make us!" yelled Henry.

"If you don't go home, I'll never speak to you as long as I live!" Beezus was really angry.

"Or me either." Mary Jane glared at the boys.

"See if we care!"

Just then Scooter rode down the street on his bicycle. "Look!" he yelled. "No hands!"

The others stopped squabbling to watch. As Scooter approached, he bent slowly backward while he continued to pedal. When his head had almost touched the fender over the back wheel, the bicycle began to wobble. The handle bars turned and the bicycle headed for the curb.

Scooter tried to sit up. It was too late. He had lost his balance. The bicycle bounced up the curb and tumbled Scooter sprawling upon the grass. The bicycle, stopped by the chestnut tree, toppled over on top of him.

Robert and Henry hooted as Scooter sheepishly untangled himself from his bicycle. He rubbed his shin but didn't say anything. The children knew the fall must have hurt, but Scooter wasn't going to admit it.

"Well, anyway, I did it once," he said, carefully feeling his right elbow to make sure it wasn't broken.

"Aw, I'll bet you didn't." Henry was pleased. Usually he was the one to have accidents while Scooter watched.

"I did, too!"

"I bet you didn't."

"Keep quiet, all of you!" shouted Beezus. "And get off my property this minute!"

"Beezus, you keep out of this!" ordered Henry.

"Aw, you're just a dumb girl," sneered Scooter.

"Yes, a dumb girl," echoed Robert. "And anyway, it isn't your property."

"My dad pays rent on it, so it's just the same as my property." Beezus raised the umbrella to hit Scooter.

"Hit him!" yelled Mary Jane, far from her usual ladylike self.

"Don't you dare hit me!"

"Hey, you kids!"

It was a strange voice. The children stopped quarreling to see who it was. A strange boy was sitting astride a bicycle by the curb. He was a big boy, big enough to be in the seventh or eighth grade. He didn't belong on Klickitat Street and none of them had ever seen him before.

"I've been yelling at you for five minutes," he said and grinned. "Is one of you Henry Huggins?"

Henry was so surprised he didn't answer. Who was this boy and how did he know his name? Robert nudged Henry, who remembered he hadn't answered. "Oh yes," he said, "that's me."

The boy reached into the pocket of his jeans and pulled out the newspaper clipping that showed Henry and Ribsy at the dog show. Henry couldn't understand why this strange boy was carrying that picture with him. Just then Ribsy began to bark furiously and Henry saw him running down the street toward them.

"Dizzy!" the boy shouted and sprang from his bicycle. "Here, Dizzy!" Ribsy jumped up on the boy and licked his hands. The boy laughed and patted him and, when Ribsy would stand still long enough, scratched him behind his left ear.

That's funny, thought Henry. How does he know Ribsy likes to be scratched behind his left ear? And why does he call him Dizzy? "His name isn't Dizzy," he said to the boy. "It's Ribsy and he's my dog!"

Ribsy looked at the boy and wagged his tail again.

A terrible thought came to Henry. Ribsy must

have belonged to the boy before he found him in the drugstore over a year ago. The boy had seen his picture in the paper and had come to take him away!

If only Ribsy hadn't won the prize in the dog show and had his picture in the paper! Then the boy would never have found him. Henry didn't know what to do. He couldn't give up Ribsy after a whole year. He couldn't.

He moved closer to Ribsy and put his hand on his collar. "He's my dog," he said. "He's my dog and you can't take him away. He was a skinny old dog when I found him and I bought him a collar and a license and a dish and now I buy him two pounds of horse meat every week and Woofies Dog Food besides. And I wash him and brush him and everything." Henry gulped. "You can't take him away!"

"Henry does take awfully good care of him," added Beezus loyally.

"Henry found him, so he must have run away

from you," said Robert.

"Finders keepers, losers weepers," chanted Mary Jane.

"Well, I had him longer than you have," said the boy. "And I fed him and brushed him, too. I had him when he was a puppy. He used to chase his tail so much I named him Dizzy. And the only reason he ran away was because he was heartbroken. I went to Scout Camp for the summer and Mom and Dad went East and we left Dizzy with my aunt and uncle. They said he was so lonesome and homesick he wouldn't eat or play or anything. Then one day they couldn't find him anywhere. They thought maybe he'd gone home to look for me so they drove over to our house to look for him. He wasn't there and they looked every place. They advertised in the paper and everything."

"So he did run away," said Robert. "You left him and he ran away."

Ribsy licked the boy's hand again.

"Look. He remembers me and wants to come home with me."

"But he likes me, too," protested Henry.

Ribsy looked at Henry and wagged his tail.

For the first time Scooter spoke. "We like Ribsy right here in this neighborhood. He's just about the most popular dog around here and every one of us would miss him."

Henry stared at Scooter in amazement. It was the first time he had heard him say anything good about Ribsy.

"Yes, we all like him," agreed Robert. "All the kids at Glenwood School like him. He waits for Henry every day under the fir tree and all the kids know him."

"Yes, what about us?" asked Beezus. "Henry has taken care of him for a whole year and I don't think it's fair for you to take him away."

"He didn't have a collar or a license tag when I found him," said Henry.

"He had them when I went off to Scout Camp.

I don't know how he lost them except my aunt said he was awfully thin when he disappeared. Maybe he slipped his collar off over his head or somebody took it." The boy reached in his pocket. "I have my birthday money that you can take." He held out a five-dollar bill to Henry.

"Five dollars! I wouldn't sell Ribsy for a million dollars!"

"Oh, I didn't mean for you to sell him," said the boy hastily. "I meant the money to help pay his expenses for the last year. I know it isn't enough, but it's all I have."

Henry felt sorry for the boy. He could understand why he would want to keep a smart dog like Ribsy. But Henry couldn't part with his dog. Nothing exciting had ever happened to him before and look at all the things that had happened this year!

Henry knelt and put his arm around his dog's neck. "You wouldn't want to leave me, would you, Ribsy? You wouldn't want to leave

Klickitat Street, would you?"

Ribsy licked Henry's face.

The stranger knelt and snapped his fingers. "Dizzy, you want to come home with me, don't you?"

Ribsy looked at him, wagged his tail, and said, "Woof!"

"I guess he likes both of us," sighed Henry. "But I don't care. He ran away from you and I found him."

"That's right. Just like I said, Finders keepers, losers weepers," said Mary Jane.

"But I raised him from a pup. And my mother and father and kid sister miss him, too."

"But he likes to meet me after school and play with the kids." Henry paused to pet the dog. Then he said slowly, "Maybe we should let Ribsy decide."

"Sure," said Scooter. "That's a good idea. Don't worry, Henry. He'll choose you."

"That seems fair enough," agreed the boy.

"How shall we let him choose?"

"I know," said Scooter. "Leave Ribsy where he is and each of you go twenty squares down the sidewalk in opposite directions. Then when I say, 'Go!' you both start calling at the same time. Whichever one Ribsy goes to gets to keep the dog."

"O.K.," agreed Henry. He felt all quivery inside.

"Sounds fair to me," agreed the boy.

"Oh, Henry, what if he doesn't choose you?" asked Beezus fearfully.

"Don't worry," said Mary Jane. "He won't want to leave Henry."

Scooter held Ribsy by his collar. Henry counted twenty squares down the sidewalk toward his house. The boy walked twenty the other way. They both turned and faced the dog. Henry's mouth felt so dry he was afraid he might not be able to call.

Scooter turned to the boy. "Say, you don't have any meat or anything in your pockets, do you?"

he asked suspiciously.

"No, I don't. Cross my heart."

"How about you, Henry?" Scooter was going to be fair.

Henry gulped. "No, me neither."

"O.K. We want to make this a fair contest."

"Good luck, Henry!" shouted Beezus.

"Thanks," said Henry weakly.

Scooter turned Ribsy toward the street so he was facing neither Henry nor the strange boy. "All right, you guys. Ready, get set—go!" He took his hand off Ribsy's collar.

"Here, Ribsy! Here, Ribsy! Come on, Ribs!" At least Henry's voice worked.

"Here, Dizzy, Dizzy, Dizzy!" The dog's former master snapped his fingers.

The dog looked at Henry. He looked at the other boy. Then he sat down to scratch behind his left ear with his left hind foot.

"Ribsy!" wailed Henry. "Come here! Here, Ribsy! Here, Ribsy!"

"Come, Dizzy! Come, Dizzy!" called the boy.

Ribsy stood up and took a few steps toward the boy and wagged his tail. The children groaned.

"Ribsy!" shouted Henry with a sinking feeling in his stomach. Ribsy stopped, turned around, wagged his tail, and said, "Woof!"

"Attaboy, Ribsy!" shouted Henry.

"Go on, Ribsy!" screamed Beezus.

"No coaching from the audience!" ordered Scooter.

Ribsy took a few steps toward Henry. Then he looked back at the other boy.

"Horse meat, Ribsy, horse meat! Here, Ribsy! Here, Ribsy!" At the mention of horse meat

Ribsy looked at Henry.

"Here, Dizzy, Dizzy!" Then the boy had an idea. "Here, Ribsy! Here, Ribsy!" he called.

"Hey, you're cheating!" objected Henry. "I'm supposed to call him Ribsy."

"There wasn't any rule about what we should call him."

"That's right, Henry," agreed Scooter.

"Look, he's turning around!" shouted Mary Jane.

But Ribsy only turned around to chew at a spot near his tail. He bit at the flea, sat down, scratched behind his left ear again, and then stood up. The boys kept on yelling.

With a tired sigh Ribsy sank down on the sidewalk, put his head on his paws, and closed his eyes.

The children groaned. "Don't go to sleep now, Ribsy!" begged Henry, who was so scared his hands felt cold and damp.

Ribsy opened his eyes and, without moving his

head, turned them first toward the strange boy and then toward Henry. "Come on, Ribsy," they both coaxed.

Slowly Ribsy stood up, and after a backward glance at the stranger, trotted eight squares down the sidewalk toward Henry. He paused, scratched again, and trotted the remaining squares to Henry. Then he sank down with his head on Henry's foot and closed his eyes again.

Ribsy had chosen Henry!

The children cheered, but Henry couldn't say a word. He knelt and hugged his dog.

"I knew he'd choose you, Henry," crowed Mary Jane. "I just knew it all the time."

"My, but I was scared for a minute," said Beezus.

The other boy looked so disappointed that Henry couldn't help feeling sorry for him. "I'm glad Ribsy wants to stay with me," said Henry, "but I'm sorry you have to lose him. He's an awfully good dog."

"I hate to lose him, too, but I guess I can't complain. It was a fair contest." The boy threw his leg over his bicycle. "Say, do you suppose I could come over to see him sometimes?"

"Sure. Any time you want."

"Thanks. I'll be around soon." The boy rode off down the street.

The children all crowded around Ribsy to pet him. "I sure am lucky," said Henry, "but he had me scared for a while."

"Jeepers, I don't know what this neighborhood would have done without Ribsy," said Beezus. "Come on. Now that Ribsy is Henry's for keeps, let's think of something we all can play."

Also by Beverly Cleary

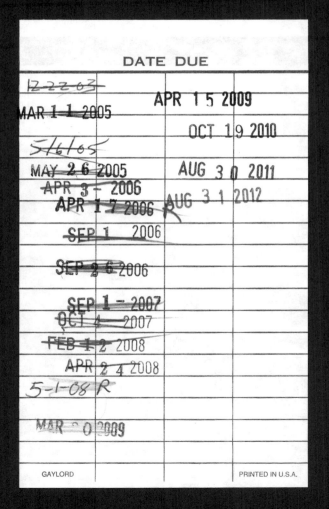